Y0-EGA-365

For my beautiful Umma
HKR

For my Sungah, Luah, and my dear grandma,
who watches over me from heaven
SL

To Yeonseo and Yoona
JK

Text copyright © 2023 by Helena Ku Rhee
Illustrations copyright © 2023 by Stella Lim and Ji-Hyuk Kim

All rights reserved. No part of this book may be reproduced, transmitted,
or stored in an information retrieval system in any form or by any means,
graphic, electronic, or mechanical, including photocopying, taping, and
recording, without prior written permission from the publisher.

First edition 2023

Library of Congress Catalog Card Number 2022906999
ISBN 978-1-5362-0993-8

23 24 25 26 27 28 TLF 10 9 8 7 6 5 4 3 2 1

Printed in Dongguan, Guangdong, China

This book was typeset in Bembo.
The illustrations were done in watercolor and finished digitally.

Candlewick Press
99 Dover Street
Somerville, Massachusetts 02144

www.candlewick.com

SORA'S SEASHELLS

Helena Ku Rhee

illustrated by Stella Lim

with Ji-Hyuk Kim

CANDLEWICK PRESS

Sora's grandmother, Halmoni, visited from far away every summer.
The day after she arrived, they took the bus to the beach, where
they combed the shore for seashells together.

They found shells with pale-pink lines, others with smooth white ridges. Some were as big as Sora's hand, others as tiny as a button.

Halmoni chose the prettiest shell and tucked it into her pocket.

On their walk to the bus stop, Halmoni placed
the shell on a bench.
"Why did you leave the shell there?" Sora asked.
"Can't we take it with us?"

"It's a gift," Halmoni said. "For anyone who sees its beauty."

Sora glanced back at the shell. She wanted to take it home, but she followed Halmoni onto the bus.

When they went back to the beach the next day, the
shell was gone.

"Halmoni," Sora said, "someone took our shell!"

"It wasn't ours. It was a gift," Halmoni said.

Sora didn't agree, but she didn't say anything.

Instead, she decided to hide some seashells
in her pockets when Halmoni wasn't watching.

By the time Halmoni left,
Sora had a jar full of shells.

A few weeks later, Sora began kindergarten. Most of the kids were nice, but a few were not.

One said, "Your name is weird!"

Another said, "Are you sure your name isn't Sara?"

Sora tried to ignore them, but her stomach hurt every time.

She didn't say anything to her parents.

But every week, the same kids teased her.

One day, a call came from far away with sad news about Halmoni.

Sora's parents explained that Halmoni was never coming back.

Sora thought of all the summers ahead without her grandmother. She remembered how Halmoni would say her name, with a soft *s* and a gently rolled *r*.

She felt sad about everything, including the mean kids at school.

All the bottled-up tears began flowing. "I want to see Halmoni,"
Sora cried. "And I hate my name. I want to be *Sara*!"

Sora's parents looked at her, and at each other.
Then the three of them went to the beach.

They walked down to the shore.

After a little while, Sora's mother picked up the most beautiful shell. It had pale-pink stripes and smooth ridges, just like Halmoni's favorites.

"*Sora* means 'seashell' in Korean," her mother said. "Halmoni always said finding a perfect shell is like receiving a wonderful gift. That's why she suggested we name you Sora."

Sora's parents held her close. "You're our greatest gift, Sora."

The next week, Sora brought her jar of seashells to school for show-and-tell. When she got up to speak, a few kids started giggling.

Sora took a deep breath. In a loud, strong voice, she said, "In Korean, *Sora* means 'seashell.' My grandmother, Halmoni, told my parents that I was a gift, just like a perfect shell, so they named me Sora."

Sora gave her
teacher a seashell.

She gave each of
her friends a shell.

Then Sora looked at the kids who teased her.

Sora gave each of them a beautiful shell.

One looked at the shell and said, "Your name makes sense now."

Another said, "Yeah, Sora sounds like a superhero name."

Sora was so surprised, she could hardly speak. "Thanks," she whispered.

Sora walked back to her seat. Her jar was almost empty, but she felt like she could fly with the seagulls.

That evening, Sora asked her parents to drive her to the beach again. She placed the last shell from her jar on the bench, as a gift for anyone who could see its beauty.